Spenser
Goes to
St. Louis

by Spenser and Mom
Illustrated by Amie Jacobsen

Text @2009 Creative Spirit Ministries, LLC
Illustrations © 2009 Amie Jacobsen

To Jessie, my brown eyed girl. May you have many exciting travels, but never forget your way back home. ~Love, Mom

Published by Simple Fish Book Company, LLC
Printed in China.

Spenser's books are produced by SpenserNation, a CSM company.

Library of Congress Cataloging-in-Publication Data

Spenser.
      Spenser goes to St. Louis / by Spenser and Mom; illustrated by Amie Jacobsen.
       p. cm.

SUMMARY: A small dog and his mother explore the history and geography of St. Louis, Missouri.
Audience: Ages 4-7
ISBN-13: 978-0-9817598-1-4
[1. St. Louis (Mo.)—Description and travel. 2. St. Louis (Mo.)—History. 3. St. Louis (Mo.)—Juvenile fiction. 4. Dogs—Juvenile fiction. 5. Travel—Juvenile fiction.] I. Title. II. Brooks, Melanie. III. Jacobsen, Amie, ill.
2009923578

For more information or additional copies, please go to www.spensernation.com.

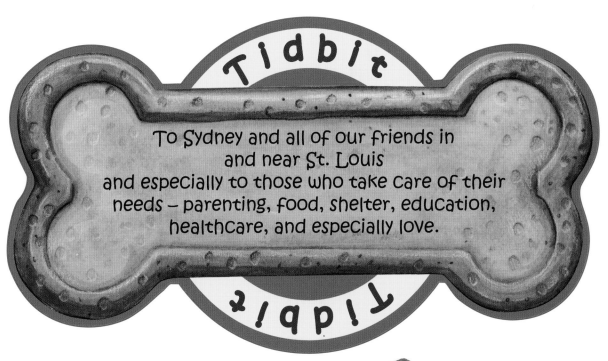

Tidbit

To Sydney and all of our friends in
and near St. Louis
and especially to those who take care of their
needs – parenting, food, shelter, education,
healthcare, and especially love.

Tidbit

Spenser and Mom

"Spenser!" Mom called, "I have great plans for this weekend. Do you want to go with me?"

Want to go with you? She never has to ask me twice. I'm always ready to go on Mom's fun trips.

"I want to go, Mom," I called, "but where are we going this time?"

"Just pack some play clothes, Spenser, and be sure to bring your baseball glove."

"My baseball glove? Why, Mom?" I asked.

"You'll find out, Spenser," was all she would tell me. She knows I love baseball!

And we were off to the airport with our suitcases and my baseball glove.

I love airplanes. Flying is so cool. We fly on really big planes. Mom gets a nice seat, and I take a little nap in my special travel bag. Mom calls me her "carry-on" because I go in my little bag right under the seat in front of her. I am very good on the plane. Mom says it is important that I don't bother any of the other passengers.

Hello, in case we haven't met before, my name is Spenser. I am a dog, but don't tell my mom that because she thinks I am a real person. Mom is always ready to go exploring and because I am her best friend, she often takes me with her.

We write a story about each city we visit. Mom likes to be sure that I learn all I can about the history, geography, and culture of the area. Do you know what culture means?

Mom had to explain it to me and it was a little hard for me to understand. "Basically," Mom said, "it's the way people live their lives and what's important to them."

Talk to your parents about your culture and get your first point.

"Okay," I thought, "I get it."

And, when Mom and I travel, we always try to find a way to help children. Mom is also teaching me how to take care of our world and so, on each trip, we have a new topic for me to learn and a new activity for me to do. I hope you will do these with me. It's always more fun to do things when you have friends that do them, too.

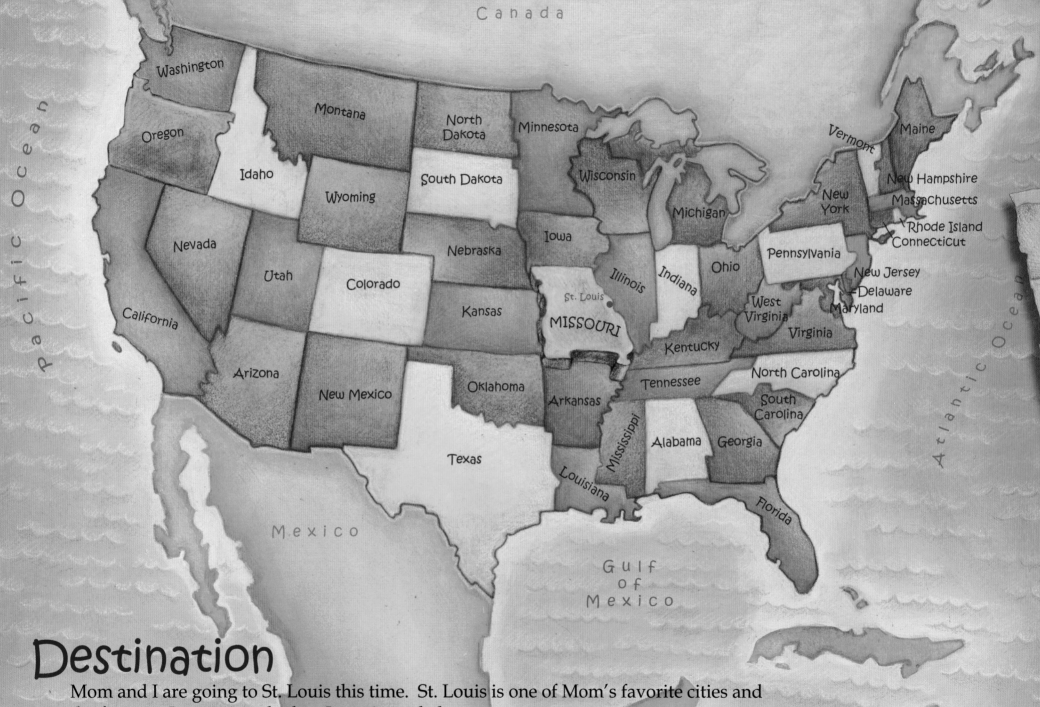

Destination

Mom and I are going to St. Louis this time. St. Louis is one of Mom's favorite cities and the first city I ever visited when I was just a baby.

St. Louis is located in the state of Missouri, which is near the middle of our country. Can you find Missouri on the map?

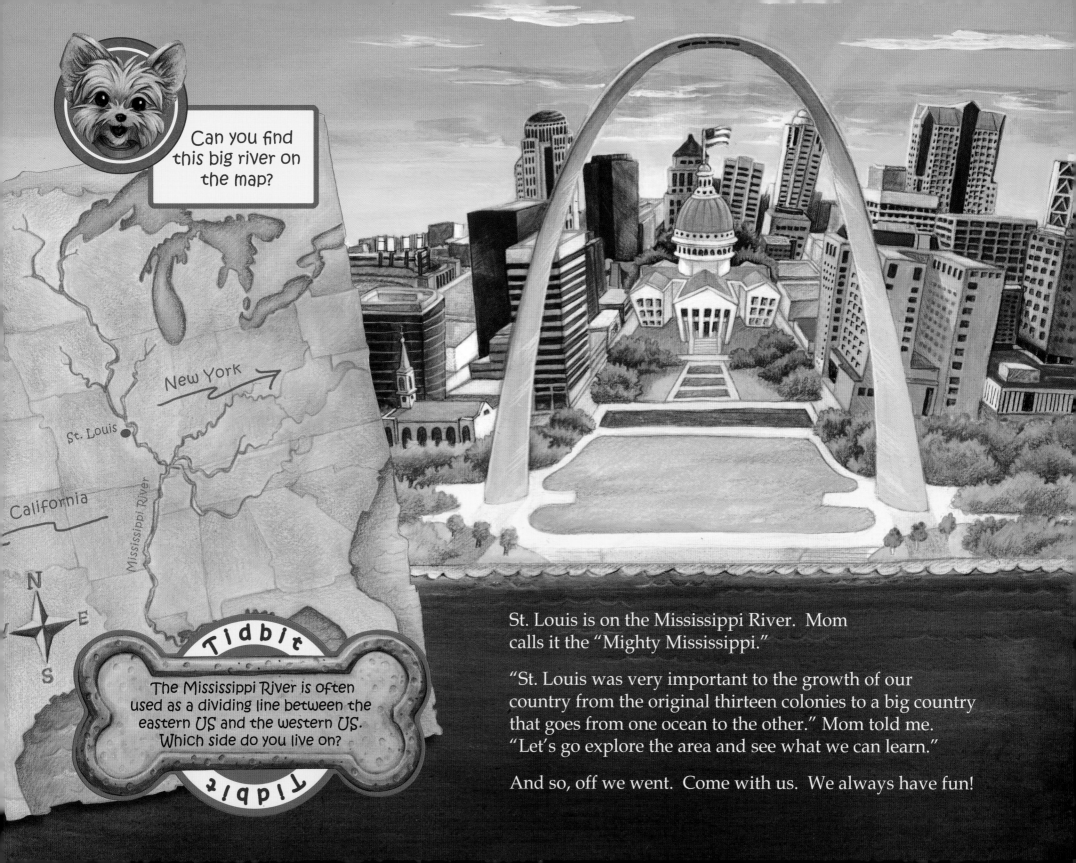

Can you find this big river on the map?

New York

St. Louis

California

Mississippi River

N
W E
S

Tidbit

The Mississippi River is often used as a dividing line between the eastern US and the western US. Which side do you live on?

St. Louis is on the Mississippi River. Mom calls it the "Mighty Mississippi."

"St. Louis was very important to the growth of our country from the original thirteen colonies to a big country that goes from one ocean to the other." Mom told me. "Let's go explore the area and see what we can learn."

And so, off we went. Come with us. We always have fun!

History

"Okay, Spenser," Mom said, "time for a little history lesson. St. Louis became part of our country when President Thomas Jefferson bought a large piece of land that was called the Louisiana Purchase. He bought the land from France, but before that it had belonged to Spain. France and Spain are countries like us.

The day that the Louisiana Purchase became part of the United States is called 'Three Flags Day.' On that day the Spanish flag was put up and taken down, then the French flag was put up and taken down, and then the American flag was put up and left flying."

"I bet that was a fun day," Spenser thought, "three flags? How cool!"

"Three Flags Day was important to the people of St. Louis, Spenser. They wanted to remember where their families had lived before coming to America. Many of their families had come from France and Spain." Mom told me.

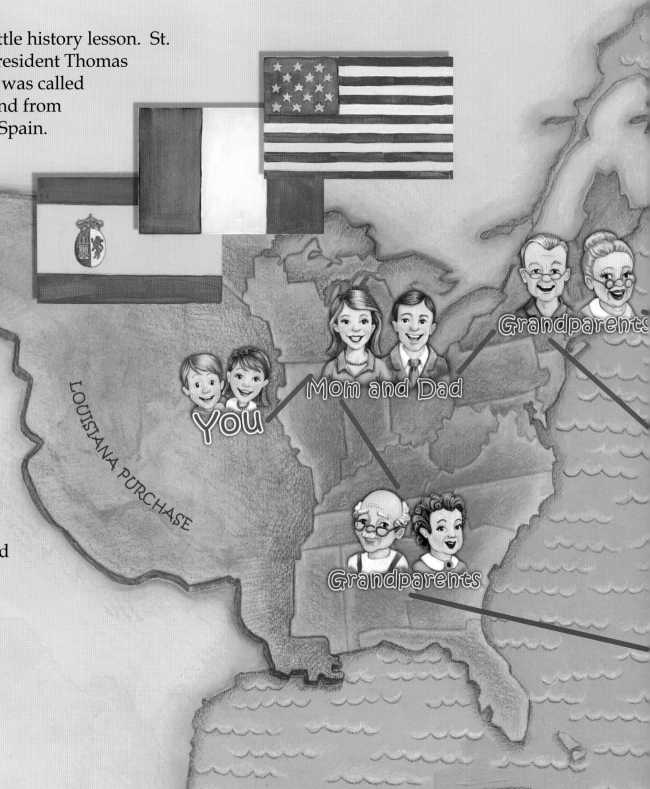

Tidbit

The Louisiana Purchase was the largest addition EVER to our country.

Tidbit

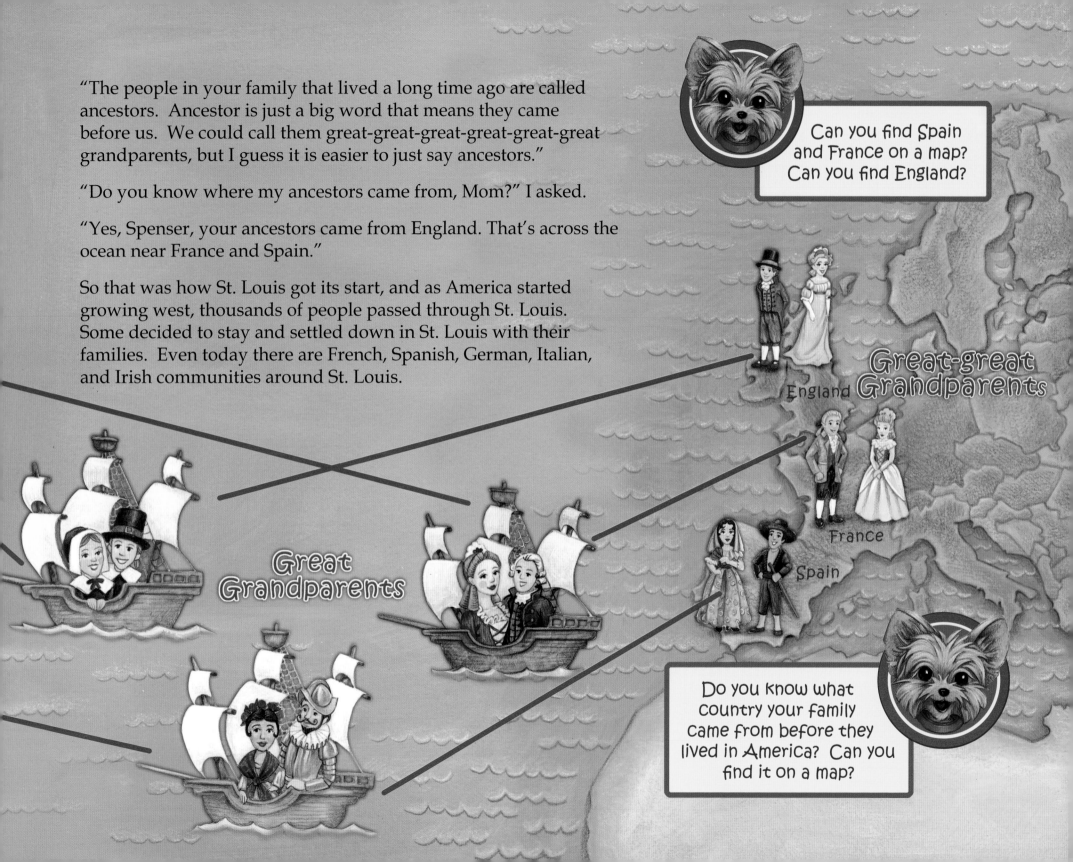

"The people in your family that lived a long time ago are called ancestors. Ancestor is just a big word that means they came before us. We could call them great-great-great-great-great-great grandparents, but I guess it is easier to just say ancestors."

"Do you know where my ancestors came from, Mom?" I asked.

"Yes, Spenser, your ancestors came from England. That's across the ocean near France and Spain."

So that was how St. Louis got its start, and as America started growing west, thousands of people passed through St. Louis. Some decided to stay and settled down in St. Louis with their families. Even today there are French, Spanish, German, Italian, and Irish communities around St. Louis.

Can you find Spain and France on a map? Can you find England?

Great-great Grandparents

England

France

Spain

Great Grandparents

Do you know what country your family came from before they lived in America? Can you find it on a map?

Is there a big river near your home? Ask your parents what activities take place on your river.

Cereal

Corn Chips

Geography

"Let's head for the river, Spenser," Mom said. "The Mississippi River is a great river. It is the second longest river in our country. It is very important for all Americans."

"Why is it important for me, Mom?" I asked, "the Mississippi River is a long way from my home."

"Yes," Mom said, "but without the Mississippi River to provide water to the middle of our country, we wouldn't have that special cereal that you love or the bread for peanut butter and jelly sandwiches. All of that food grows because we have the Mighty Mississippi – food for us and food to send to other countries all over the world."

"Now you're talking," Spenser said, "anything that helps my tummy must be important."

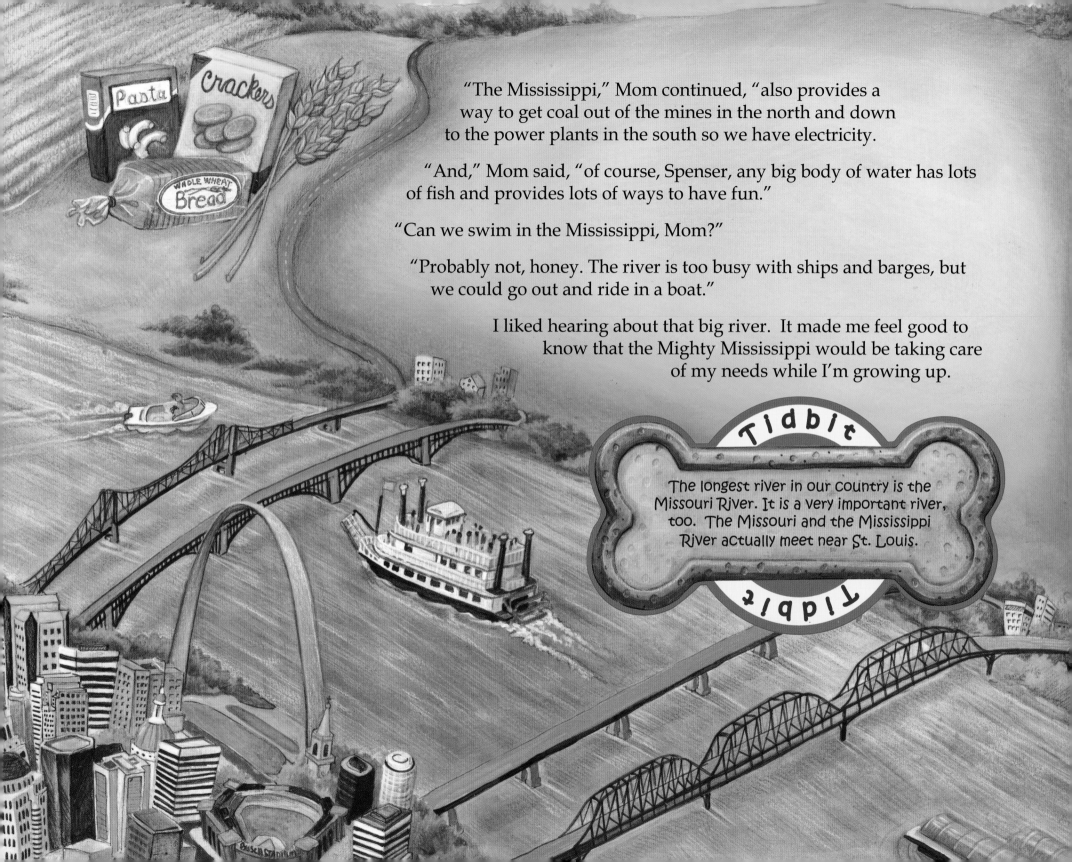

"The Mississippi," Mom continued, "also provides a way to get coal out of the mines in the north and down to the power plants in the south so we have electricity.

"And," Mom said, "of course, Spenser, any big body of water has lots of fish and provides lots of ways to have fun."

"Can we swim in the Mississippi, Mom?"

"Probably not, honey. The river is too busy with ships and barges, but we could go out and ride in a boat."

I liked hearing about that big river. It made me feel good to know that the Mighty Mississippi would be taking care of my needs while I'm growing up.

Tidbit

The longest river in our country is the Missouri River. It is a very important river, too. The Missouri and the Mississippi River actually meet near St. Louis.

Science

"I have a special surprise, Spensey," Mom said.

Surprise? I love surprises! "What kind of surprise?" I asked Mom. "Is it something to eat?"

"Even better, we are going to see some special animals."

Wow! I love animals (maybe because I am one!). "A zoo, Mom?" I asked.

"Even better, Spenser" Mom said again. "We are going to see three very different kinds of animals – all in places similar to their natural homes."

We drove over to the Illinois side of the big river, stopped the car, got out, and walked down towards the water. It was wet and cold. There, in the ice floating in the river, were some of the most beautiful birds I'd ever seen. They had white heads and yellow beaks and feet, but their bodies were dark brown.

Tidbit

The Bald Eagle is the national bird of the US. The only place in the world that you can find a bald eagle is in North America.

"What are they, Mom?" I asked.

"American bald eagles," Mom said. "This is one of the few places in the country where eagles come to rest each year."

"Wow! Look, Mom!" I shouted as I slipped and tumbled my way down to the water's edge.

"I know you're excited, but you need to calm down a little," Mom said. She knows how excited I get when I see or learn new things. Eagles are the coolest birds ever – and they are very big!

Ask your parents or teachers to show you a picture of an eagle.

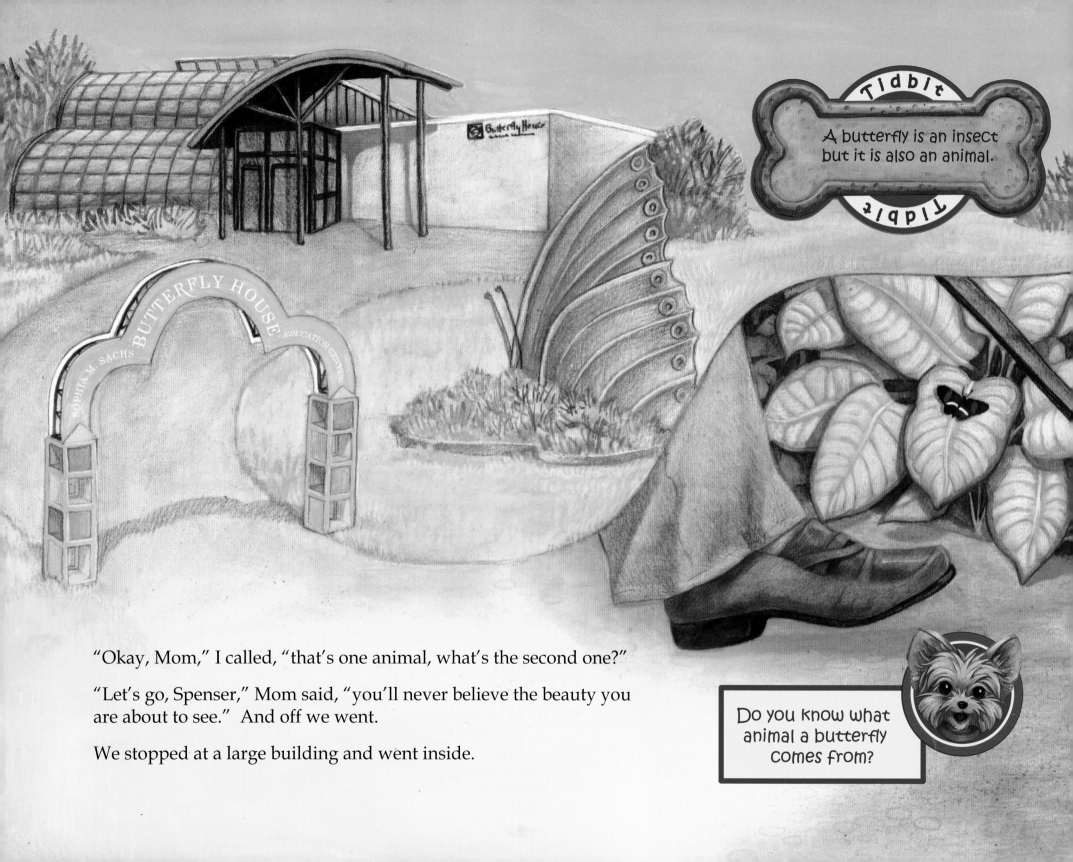

"Okay, Mom," I called, "that's one animal, what's the second one?"

"Let's go, Spenser," Mom said, "you'll never believe the beauty you are about to see." And off we went.

We stopped at a large building and went inside.

Do you know what animal a butterfly comes from?

"Oh, my gosh, Mom!" I yelled, "there are jillions of them!"

Well, maybe not jillions or even thousands but certainly hundreds of beautiful butterflies in St. Louis' Butterfly House. The Butterfly House is a place where people go to learn about butterflies.

"Can I take one home?" I asked.

Tidbit

Butterflies spread their wings and take sunbaths to store up enough heat and energy to be able to fly.

Tidbit

Can you name some other insects? (Hint: sometimes we call them bugs.)

"No," Mom said, "butterflies need to live in this beautiful place that has been built for them. We can't take them away from their families but if you come over here, you can let one land on your back."

And it did – it landed right on my back. It even tickled a little!

I am really puzzled now. What could the third animal be? We've seen the great American bald eagle, and we've seen beautiful butterflies. What other exciting animal could Mom find in St. Louis?

Mom pulled up beside a sign. "What does that say?" she asked.

I sounded out the words carefully – "GRANT'S FARM." A farm? I've been to farms lots of times, and I love cows and pigs and chickens, but Mom said this was going to be different.

"Okay, Mom," I said, "I give up. What is special about this farm?"

And just as I said it, we drove around a corner and there, in front of me, were the biggest horses I had ever seen.

"These are the world-famous Clydesdales," Mom explained. "They are much bigger than the regular horses that you see at home. A Clydesdale can weigh as much as a Volkswagen Beetle, and their main job is to pull heavy wagons so their legs are very strong.

The Clydesdales live here at Grant's Farm. This special farm provides a home for these beautiful horses and their families."

Have you ever been to a farm? If not, ask your parents or your teachers to tell you all about farms.

Tidbit

Clydesdales have lots of hair, usually white, on their legs. This hair is called feather. I think this is funny because birds have feathers, too. Can you imagine a big horse using his feathers to fly?

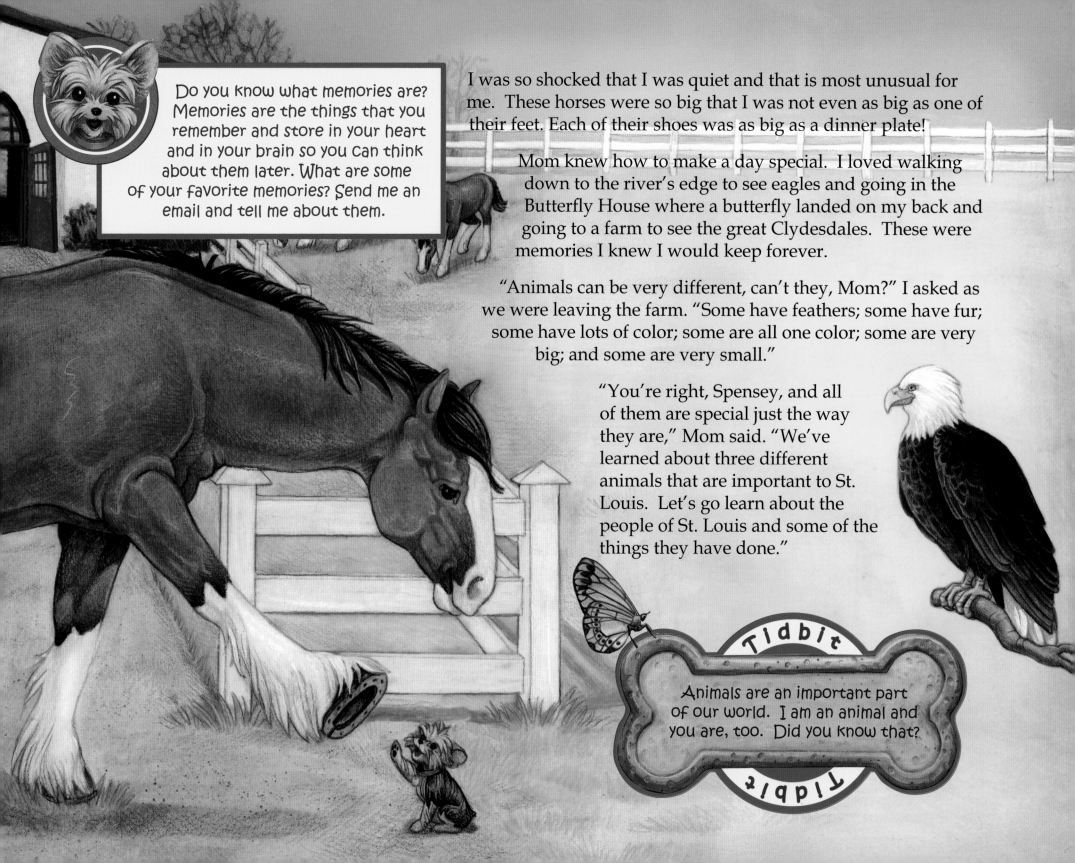

Do you know what memories are? Memories are the things that you remember and store in your heart and in your brain so you can think about them later. What are some of your favorite memories? Send me an email and tell me about them.

I was so shocked that I was quiet and that is most unusual for me. These horses were so big that I was not even as big as one of their feet. Each of their shoes was as big as a dinner plate!

Mom knew how to make a day special. I loved walking down to the river's edge to see eagles and going in the Butterfly House where a butterfly landed on my back and going to a farm to see the great Clydesdales. These were memories I knew I would keep forever.

"Animals can be very different, can't they, Mom?" I asked as we were leaving the farm. "Some have feathers; some have fur; some have lots of color; some are all one color; some are very big; and some are very small."

"You're right, Spensey, and all of them are special just the way they are," Mom said. "We've learned about three different animals that are important to St. Louis. Let's go learn about the people of St. Louis and some of the things they have done."

Tidbit

Animals are an important part of our world. I am an animal and you are, too. Did you know that?

Tidbit

Culture

"Well, a long time ago," Mom said, "St. Louis was chosen to have a very special event - the World's Fair."

I was listening very carefully. I know about fairs and I know that they are fun, but I wasn't sure about a World's Fair. It sounds pretty big.

"What is a World's Fair, Mom?" I asked.

Mom explained, "A World's Fair is when people come from all over the world to teach others about their countries. There is good food and entertainment and lots of education.

Many food stories came out of the St. Louis World's Fair, Spenser. Some people say the ice cream cone was invented when someone ran out of cups for ice cream. It was also said that the St. Louis World's Fair was the first place a sausage was placed on bread and served with ketchup and mustard. Today we call that a hot dog."

Tidbit

This World's Fair was especially important to St. Louis because it was the 100th birthday of the Louisiana Purchase.

"Hmmmm," I thought, "now that's a good idea. Hot dogs and ice cream are two of my favorite foods."

"No, silly," Mom said, "the St. Louis World's Fair was over a long time ago. We can't get ice cream and hot dogs there today, but we can look at the beautiful park and the lakes that were made for the Fair."

Talk about a "getting lost" plan with your parents. What should you do?

Yeah, that means I get off my leash and can run free! But I'm pretty good and stay close to Mom. Our rule is that I must always be able to see her. Do you have rules like that with your parents when you go somewhere in public? It is very important not to get lost or go off by yourself.

"I think I would like to go to a World's Fair, Mom," I said.

"Well, maybe one day you can," Mom answered. "The next World's Fair will be in China, and I think that is a little too far away."

Can you find China on a map or globe?

"Spensey," Mom called, and woke me out of a little nap. "I have a surprise. Close your eyes."

Another surprise! I love surprises so I was instantly wide-awake. What could she be talking about? Was I finally going to get that ice cream and a hot dog?

"Okay, open your eyes!" Mom leaned over me and said, "What do you see?"

And what do you think I saw? What do I love almost as much as ice cream and traveling with Mom? Baseball! A big new baseball stadium!

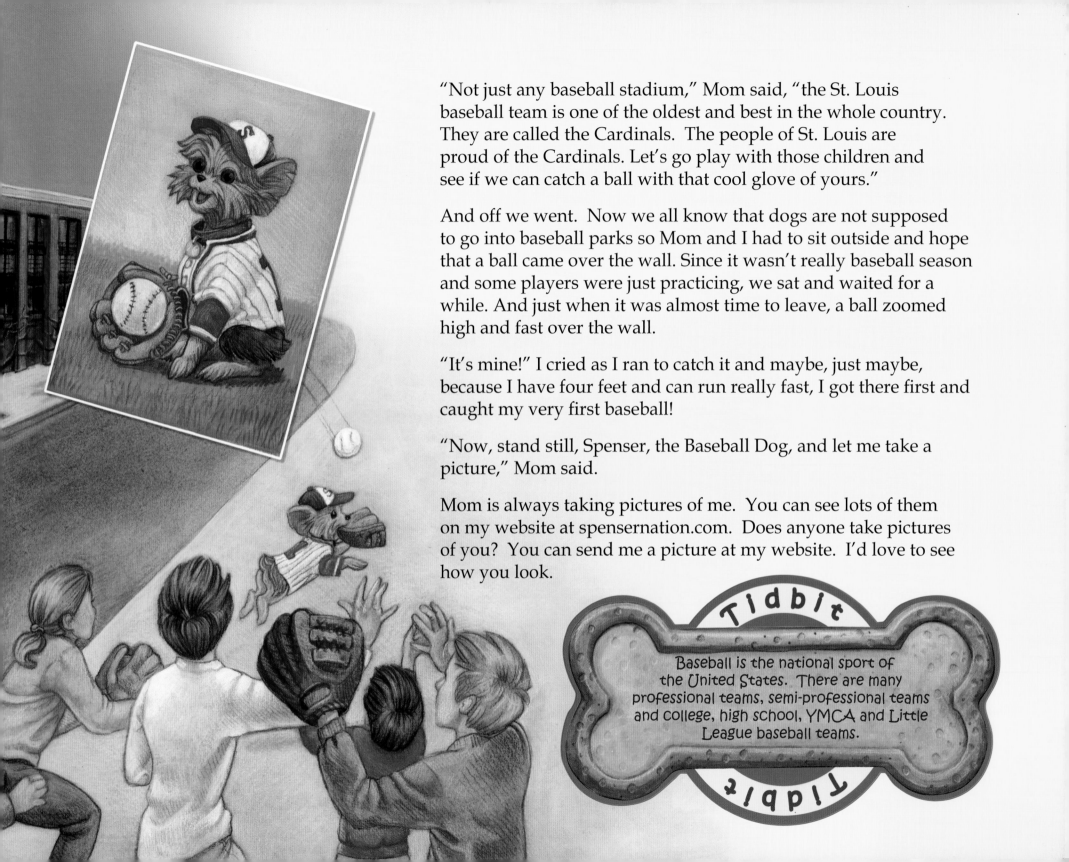

"Not just any baseball stadium," Mom said, "the St. Louis baseball team is one of the oldest and best in the whole country. They are called the Cardinals. The people of St. Louis are proud of the Cardinals. Let's go play with those children and see if we can catch a ball with that cool glove of yours."

And off we went. Now we all know that dogs are not supposed to go into baseball parks so Mom and I had to sit outside and hope that a ball came over the wall. Since it wasn't really baseball season and some players were just practicing, we sat and waited for a while. And just when it was almost time to leave, a ball zoomed high and fast over the wall.

"It's mine!" I cried as I ran to catch it and maybe, just maybe, because I have four feet and can run really fast, I got there first and caught my very first baseball!

"Now, stand still, Spenser, the Baseball Dog, and let me take a picture," Mom said.

Mom is always taking pictures of me. You can see lots of them on my website at spensernation.com. Does anyone take pictures of you? You can send me a picture at my website. I'd love to see how you look.

Tidbit

Baseball is the national sport of the United States. There are many professional teams, semi-professional teams and college, high school, YMCA and Little League baseball teams.

Lending a Paw

The next morning Mom and I were lazy. I played with my baseball, and she read the paper.

After a while Mom said, "We have had so much fun in St. Louis that it is time for us to give something back to this wonderful place. I've heard about a special project in St. Louis, called Scouting for Food, which helps feed hungry children. Come on, Spenser, let's go see what we can learn."

Operation Hungry Child is what Mom calls her pet project. She says she named it for me because I am always hungry, but I know she named it for the hungry children that are found in every city in America. Mom and I are working hard to make sure hungry children get good meals.

In each city we visit, we take time to find someone who is feeding children and we help out.

"Let's go," Mom said, and we headed off to the Kirkwood Fire Station.

"Listen, Spenser, and let me tell you about the Scouting for Food program," Mom said. "In November each year, the Boy Scouts go door-to-door in St. Louis leaving empty plastic bags. The next weekend they go back and pick them up and deliver them to the local fire department.

Tidbit

The Scouting for Food program started in St. Louis and has been adopted by other food banks around our country.

The firemen help the Scouts pack the food in boxes to deliver to the St. Louis Food Bank. Last year the Scouts collected over 2,000,000 pounds of food. We won't be here for the November food drive, but maybe we can find a way to help out today."

Mom and I met some Boy Scouts and some firemen when we got to the Fire Station. They were making plans for an even bigger food drive next year.

"This story is all about numbers," the Scout leader told Mom and me. "30,000 Scouts do the work. 10,000 volunteers help them. 1,300,000 bags are distributed. 43,000 boxes are packed with food. 49 fire stations help the Scouts. And hungry children in 7 counties receive food from this drive."

"These are the kind of numbers Mom likes," I thought. "Could you add two more people to those numbers?" I asked the Scout leader. "Mom and I would really like to help. Can we come back in November, Mom, pretty please?"

"We'll try our best, sweet Spensey," Mom said. "It does sound like a great way to spend a weekend."

Can you add up all of those numbers? Make sure to start with the 2,000,000 pounds of food.

Tidbit

Boy Scouts and firemen both have a tradition of serving others.

Tidbit

A Special Treat

Mom and I loved meeting with the Scouts and the firemen. What great people they are!

"Let's head downtown," Mom said, "so I can show you something that you can find only in St. Louis."

"Eagles?" I'm thinking, "or Clydesdales, or hundreds of butterflies? I've already seen all of those."

"Look," Mom said, and pointed upward.

"What is that thing, Mom?" I asked as I craned my neck backwards to look way up in the sky.

"That's called the Gateway Arch. St. Louis built it to represent all of the people who passed through the city on their way out west. It is the tallest monument in the country – twice as tall as the Statue of Liberty and even taller than the Washington Monument."

"Can we go up in it, Mom?" I asked. My tail was wagging – this looked like so much fun.

"Sorry, Spense, only people are allowed in the arch, but yes, they can go all the way to the top and look out those little windows up there. They can see the baseball stadium and up and down that big river."

Tidbit

A million people a year go to the top of the arch to look out of those little windows. Some people even get married up there.

If you've been to the top of the arch, I wish you would write me at my website and tell me about it. If you haven't been able to go, check it out on the internet or in an encyclopedia.

Poor, poor me – sometimes dogs have to miss out on all the fun. But at least you can go up there if you ever visit St. Louis.

"How about some frozen custard, Spensey?" Mom asked.

"What is that, Mom?"

"It's like ice cream, only better. Frozen custard is a St. Louis tradition, and the best place to get it is at Ted Drewes. Let's go."

And, yes, it was good. Some people call this frozen custard, concrete, because you can turn the cup upside down and it doesn't fall out.

It had been a great day but a long one. I was ready to go to bed.

TED D

Taking Care Of Our World

Mom and I were on our way home. It had been another excellent adventure, and Mom even let me carry my baseball and glove on the airplane.

"Mom," I said, "don't forget my green lesson." A "green lesson" is what I call it when Mom is teaching me about taking care of our earth. We talk about these sometimes on the plane; sometimes riding in the car; whenever we get a chance.

"Spenser," Mom said, "you know we would never forget something that important. Today, let's talk about saving electricity. Turning off lights when we're not using them is something you could do that would save electricity."

"What's the big deal about turning off lights, Mom?" I asked.

Make a chart to hang in your room. Mark on it every time you forget to turn off your light. Talk to your parents about ways to help you remember.

"Well, some of our natural resources are used to make electricity, so if we save on electricity, we save our natural resources. The big word for this is 'conservation'."

"I can do this," I said, thinking of all of the times I have left my bedroom light on when I went to play. "Mom, can one little light bulb make a difference?"

"Yes, of course," Mom said. "If we all turned off a light bulb, think how much energy we would save."

That settled it. Another problem I could work on. "I will turn my light off every time I'm not using it, Mom," I promised.

"And I will try harder to turn things off too, Spense. It's a deal," Mom said.

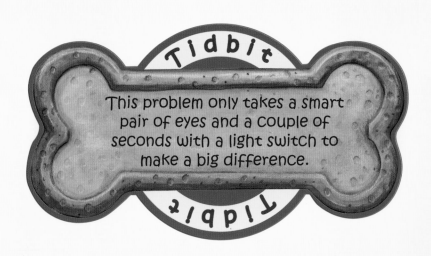

Tidbit

This problem only takes a smart pair of eyes and a couple of seconds with a light switch to make a big difference.

Tidbit

As I put my glove and baseball away back home in my bedroom, I thought about the Mighty Mississippi River and I thought about eagles, butterflies, and really big horses. I thought about World's Fairs with ice cream cones and hot dogs and baseball stadiums with balls that fly over the wall. I also thought about Scouting for Food and how much the Boy Scouts and firemen do to help hungry children. And I thought about how Mom had taught me to conserve electricity. What a busy trip it had been, and what great memories I had! I loved St. Louis and its all-the-way-up-to-the-sky arch and concrete ice cream. I knew we would visit again.

"Thank you, Mom, for taking me back to St. Louis," I said, as I got into bed.

"You're welcome, my sweet Spensey," Mom replied as she kissed me good night. "I love exploring with you, and St. Louis is a very special place to explore. Would you want to go back?"

"You bet," I said, as my eyes closed, "St. Louis is way cool! Don't forget November, Mom."

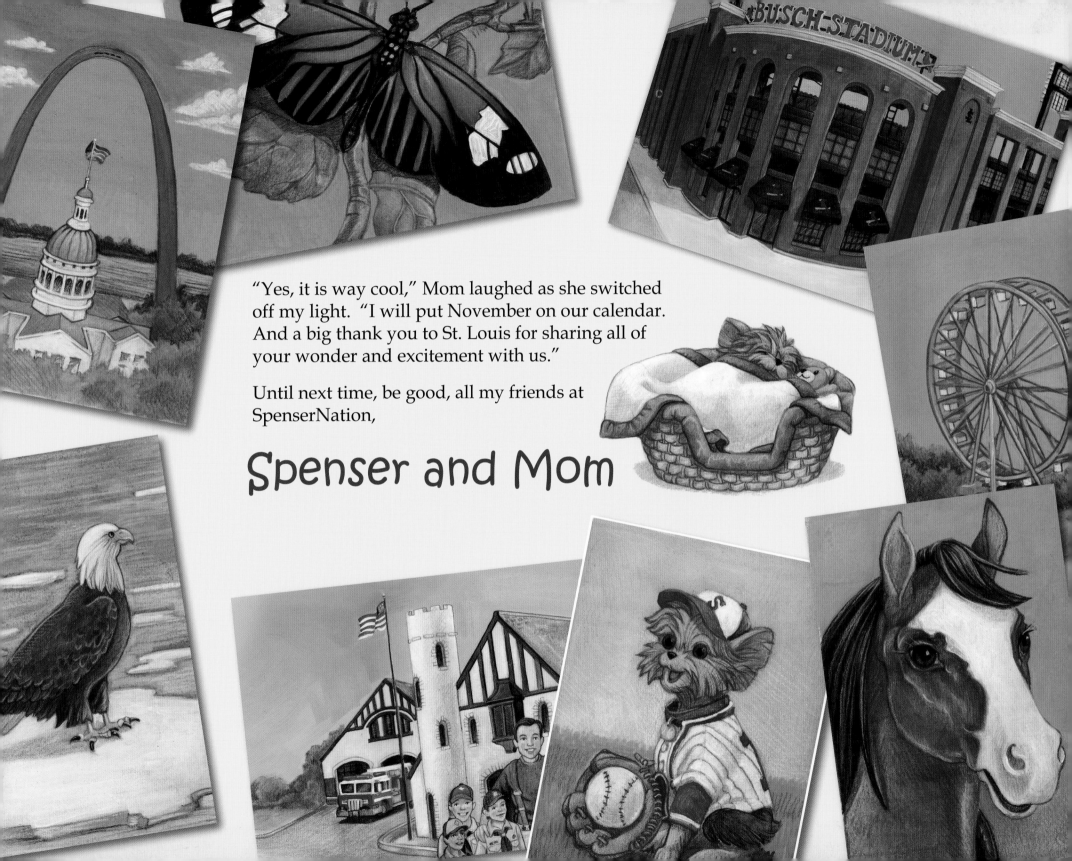

"Yes, it is way cool," Mom laughed as she switched off my light. "I will put November on our calendar. And a big thank you to St. Louis for sharing all of your wonder and excitement with us."

Until next time, be good, all my friends at SpenserNation,

Spenser and Mom

Foodbank
St. Louis Area Foodbank

About St. Louis Area Foodbank

The St. Louis Area Foodbank is driven by its mission to feed hungry people by acquiring and distributing food through our member agencies, and educate the public about the nature of and the solutions to the problems of hunger. St. Louis Area Foodbank collects and distributes food to 500+ food pantries, soup kitchens and shelters throughout 14 counties in Missouri and 12 counties in Illinois.

We help...

the elderly, single-parent families and the working poor. Children comprise the largest segment of the population in need of food. Hunger does not discriminate. It affects poor and homeless people in urban and rural areas.

We rely...

on the generosity of others. More than 8,000 volunteers, contributing over 24,000 hours, help sort and pack food; area food companies, grocery stores and government sources donate food; businesses, group and individuals organize or contribute to successful food drives and provide financial support the Foodbank needs to ensure that the hungry receive balanced meals.